Off to Scho with Periwinkle and Blue

adapted by Alison Inches
based on the teleplay by Alice Wilder
illustrated by Jennifer Oxley

Simon Spotlight/Nick Jr.
New York   London   Toronto   Sydney   Singapore

Based on the TV series *Blue's Clues*®, created by Traci Paige Johnson, Todd Kessler, and Angela C. Santomero as seen on Nick Jr.®
On *Blue's Clues*, Joe is played by Donovan Patton. Photos by Joan Marcus.

SIMON SPOTLIGHT
An imprint of Simon & Schuster Children's Publishing Division
1230 Avenue of the Americas, New York, New York 10020
Copyright © 2003 Viacom International Inc.
SIMON SPOTLIGHT and colophon are registered trademarks of Simon & Schuster.
Manufactured in the United States of America
ISBN 0-689-85498-6
First Edition   10 9 8 7 6 5 4 3 2 1

It was Periwinkle's first day of school.

"I'm really excited!" he said to Blue and Joe. "But I'm a little nervous, too."

He was glad that they were coming with him.

"Let's go!" Periwinkle said as he hopped out the door.
"*To school we go, to school we go—it's off to school we go!*" they sang as they walked.

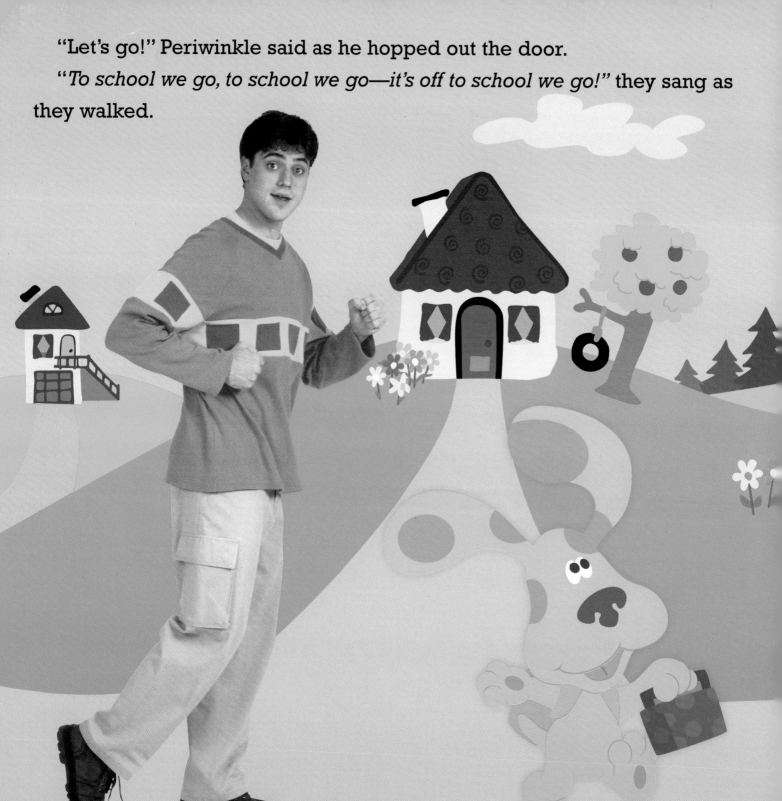

But when Periwinkle saw his school, he stopped singing.

"Will school be okay?" he asked.

"I have a great time at school," said Blue.

But Periwinkle still wasn't sure about school. He wondered what the classroom would be like. Would his teacher be nice? Would he make new friends?

"What if I don't like school?" asked Periwinkle.

"Well," said Joe thoughtfully, "do you like to paint pictures? Or read stories? Or build things with blocks?"

"Yes," said Periwinkle. "I like to do all those things!"

"Then I bet you're going to *love* school!" said Joe.

In the classroom Periwinkle's teacher introduced herself. "Welcome to school, Periwinkle. I'm Miss Marigold," she said. Then she asked Blue to show Periwinkle the cubbies.

"Which one is mine?" asked Periwinkle.

"The one with your picture on it," said Blue.

Periwinkle looked at all the cubbies. "Hey, that's me!" he exclaimed when he saw his picture.

Blue and Periwinkle put their lunch boxes in their cubbies.

Miss Marigold clapped her hands. "Okay, it's Circle Time!" she said.
"Let's all sit in a circle on the rug." Periwinkle sat next to Blue.

"We have someone new today," said Miss Marigold.

"This is Periwinkle."

"Hi, Periwinkle!" said the whole class, smiling at him.

Periwinkle blinked and smiled back.

"It's time to play the name game," said Miss Marigold. "Pick a color from the pile. Then say your name and your favorite color."

Blue went first. "I'm Blue, and blue is my favorite color!" she said.

Next it was Periwinkle's turn. "I'm Periwinkle! And my favorite color is red!" he said.

"Red is my favorite color too!" said Purple Kangaroo.

Wow, thought Periwinkle. Someone likes the same thing I like!

After Circle Time, Periwinkle learned that everyone had a special job. Periwinkle looked at the job board and saw that his job was to feed Giggles, the rabbit.

"I've never fed a rabbit before," said Periwinkle. "I'm not sure what to do."

"There's a sign above the cage," Miss Marigold said.

Periwinkle looked at the sign. "It says Giggles gets three cups of food."

"That's right," said Miss Marigold, and they measured the pellets together.

"One, two, three!" exclaimed Periwinkle as he put the pellets in Giggles's cage.

At recess everyone went outside. The playground had lots of great stuff—even a water table. Periwinkle liked to race the boats and splash them into the water.

"Stop it, Periwinkle!" said Orange Kitten. "You're getting us all wet!"

Periwinkle looked at his wet classmates.

"Sorry," said Periwinkle. "I'll try to be more careful."

After that they all had a better time at the water table.

When they came inside it was time to paint. But Periwinkle wanted to play with blocks.

"Right now it's Painting Time," said Miss Marigold.

"But I *really* want to play with blocks," said Periwinkle.

"You can play with blocks tomorrow," said Miss Marigold. She pointed to the schedule. "Can you tell me what it's time for now?" she asked.

"It's time to paint!" Periwinkle said excitedly. He put on a smock and swished paint across his paper. Then Joe walked in to check on Periwinkle.

"That's a nice painting," said Joe.

"Thanks," said Periwinkle. "It's Painting Time!"

At lunch Periwinkle sat at the lunch table with his classmates. They all had different things in their lunch boxes.

"I have a brownie!" said Green Puppy.

"I have a cookie!" said Periwinkle.

"Want to trade desserts?" asked Green Puppy.

"Sure!" said Periwinkle.

Then it was time to go home.

"But I don't want to go home!" said Periwinkle.

"You don't?" said Joe. "That must mean you liked school."

"I did! I liked it ALL! School is cool!" said Periwinkle.

"And I can't wait to come back tomorrow!"